Cat and Dog

For Tess and Matthew

Cat and Dog

Peta Coplans

Hodder
Children's
Books

a division of Hodder Headline plc

First published in Great Britain in 1995 by Andersen Press Ltd.
20 Vauxhall Bridge Road, London SW1V 2SA.
Paperback edition first published in 1997 by
Hodder Children's Books,
338 Euston Road, London NW1 3BH.
All rights reserved. Colour separated in Switzerland
by Photolitho AG, Offsetreproduktionen, Gossau, Zurich.
Printed and bound in Hong Kong

10   9   8   7   6   5   4   3   2   1

British Library Cataloguing in Publication Data available.

ISBN 0 340 68161 6

A dog was walking along the beach.
It was a hot and sunny day,
just the weather for a swim.

As he strolled down to the sea
he saw a cat unpacking a
picnic basket.

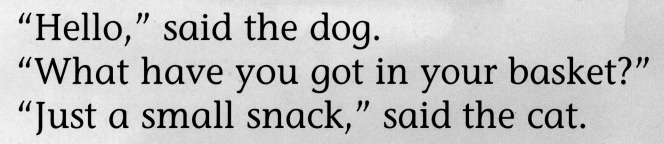

"Hello," said the dog.
"What have you got in your basket?"
"Just a small snack," said the cat.

The dog went off to swim,
but afterwards he felt hungry.
The cat was about to eat
a large picnic lunch.

"May I join you?" said the dog.
"I'm very hungry."
"Oh no," said the cat.
"This is all for me."

"We could play a game," said the dog.
"I know a good one."
"How do you play?" asked the cat.

"Look up," said the dog.
"How many butterflies can you see?"

"One," said the cat.
So the dog sneaked one tiny cake.

"How many castles on the sand?"
asked the dog.
"Two," said the cat, standing up.

So the dog swallowed
two small fishes.

"How many birds can you see
on the rocks?" asked the dog.

"Three," said the cat, walking away.
So the dog munched three
fresh tomatoes.

"How many divers can you see in the water?" asked the dog. "Four," called the cat.

So the dog nibbled four
cucumber sandwiches.

"Can you see any waves?"
asked the dog.
"Yes, five," called the cat,
splashing in the water.

So the dog wolfed down
five red strawberries.

"Tell me what else you can
see," said the dog.
"I see six white clouds in
the sky," said the cat.

"Good," said the dog,
as he crunched
six potato
crisps.

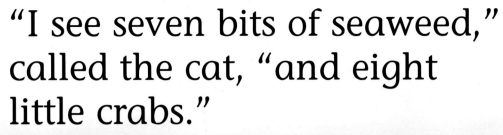

"I see seven bits of seaweed," called the cat, "and eight little crabs."

"Very good," said the dog. And he guzzled seven little sausages and eight ring doughnuts.

The cat came running back.
"Look!" she shouted.
"I found nine starfish."

"Great," said the dog, gobbling
nine little crackers.

"Hey," said the cat,
"where's my lunch?"
"Only ten wrinkly raisins left,"
said the dog. "And when I've
eaten those I'm coming to get you."

"You'll never catch me," said the cat.
"You've had too much to eat."

"Want to play again tomorrow?"